The Secret Under the Staircase

by I.M. Lerner & Catherine L. Osornio

illustrated by Melissa Leonard

D1319625

An Under the Staircase™ Book

To my wonderful husband, Ben, the love of my life.
To my Maya and Nate, you are truly gifts from God.
To my loving parents for your unconditional love and support.
To the best sibs a middle kid could ever have. Seriously, you guys.
And to the army of supporters who helped bring this series to life. There's so much at stake.

I.M.L.

To my four children, Noah, Nathan, Ruth, and Rachel, who love this country and value the principles upon which it was founded.

C.L.O.

Design and layout by Todd Pierce, Rachel Skybetter, Fred Schaaf, and the amazing crew at BatesMeron (batesmeron.com).

Under the Staircase Books
P.O. Box 3833
Reston, VA 20195
underthestaircase.com
read@underthestaircase.com

Special discounts are available on quantity purchases. For details, contact the publisher at the address above.

This book is a work of fiction. Names, characters, places, and incidents either are products of the author's imagination or are used fictitiously. Any resemblance to actual persons, living or dead, events, or locales is entirely coincidental.

Printed in the United States of America
First Edition
Library of Congress Control Number: 2013923169
ISBN-13 978-0-9913187-0-4 (paperback)
ISBN-13 978-0-9913187-1-1 (MOBI)
ISBN-13 978-0-9913187-2-8 (ePUB)

PROLOGUE
LONDON – MARCH 1775

The sound was ever so slight—hardly recognizable as a knock. But the elderly man, despite his age, was quick to open the door.

He quietly ushered the visitor into the entryway. "You have not been followed?" he asked.

The visitor noted several men at the other end of the room who were wrapping books and stamping packages by candlelight; their reflections cast eerie shadows against the wall. "I took precautions," the visitor told the older man, "though I do not see the need. We have been seen together before."

"Yes, my friend," the older man said. "But caution is always a necessity, especially when liberty is threatened."

"Then it is true?" the visitor asked. "The negotiations have broken down?"

THE SECRET UNDER THE STAIRCASE

The older man nodded, his glasses flashing as they reflected the light from the lantern on the nearby table. "We could be at war any time. That is why I must leave."

The visitor pulled off the satchel that was slung over his shoulder and reached inside. He pulled out a thick stack of papers that was tied together with a string. "This is all I could do on such short notice. 'Tisn't finished yet. I hope it will help."

"It will do much good," the older man said, taking the bundle and placing it in his traveling bag. "I will guard this with my life. Thank you."

The visitor shook the older man's hand. "I will miss you, my friend. I doubt that I will ever cross the pond, especially if there is war."

The older man gently tapped his bag. "You will travel with me in word. This kind of freedom will flourish…it must flourish. Our very lives depend upon it."

The visitor nodded then silently walked out the door. The older man latched it behind him.

Snuffing out the nearby lantern, the older man moved toward the window. He opened the curtain ever so slightly and peered out, watching as his friend walked down the street and turned the corner. So far, so good. There didn't seem to be anyone following.

THE SECRET UNDER THE STAIRCASE

He sighed deeply and closed the curtain, thinking of the papers now in his possession. Their plans must succeed. He closed his eyes for a brief moment, realizing the weight that had just been placed upon his shoulders.

"Sir?" a voice called behind him. "We are finished. Shall we start distributing the packages?"

The older man opened his eyes. He turned toward the young man and nodded. "Yes. Go forth through the secret passageway: one, then two at a time. Be on your guard. Just because we have seen no sign of them, does not mean they are not watching. Now is the time we must be most vigilant."

The young man nodded and returned to the others. Then quietly they left, one, then two at a time, each clutching a package.

"Godspeed," the older man whispered as the last man slipped through the passageway. The early rays of dawn crept in through the window. As he glanced out into the silent street, he knew the society was on the move. In just a few hours he would be on the move, too, sailing across the sea, toward home and toward an uncertain future.

Would these papers help? He could only hope and pray it would be so. He turned back into the room, hoping to get an hour or two of sleep.

PROLOGUE

He never saw the man in black, hidden in the shadows in the alley across the street, watching his window in silence. He never saw the smile that settled on the man's face as he disappeared into the depths of the city.

CHAPTER ONE
KIRKCALDY POINT, VIRGINIA – PRESENT

"Grandma! Grandpa! Where are you?" twelve-year-old Maya Liber called up the stairway as she and her brother, Nate, who had just turned ten, entered their grandparents' house and store, the Library Café. "We're back!"

Grandma Georgia hurried down the first flight of stairs and scooped her two grandchildren into her arms, her long gray-black hair, usually tucked neatly into a bun at the back of her head, was beginning to unravel. "Oooh! I missed you two so much! How was your trip?"

"Great!" Nate said as he picked up his bags and headed up to the third floor residence. "We went all over—San Francisco, Sacramento, San Antonio, Chicago, Gettysburg, Boston, Philadelphia, Jamestown—but I'm glad to be back in good old Kirkcaldy Point-on-the-Potomac. Did you get our postcards?"

Grandma nodded as she picked up one of Maya's bags and followed Nate upstairs. "Yes. And thank you for sending them. I know you must think it's a bit old fashioned, but I still like receiving them in the mail. We especially loved the one from Gunston Hall, although that one is just down the river."

"I picked that one," Maya said. "I'm glad you liked it. Where's Grandpa?"

Grandma frowned, her brown eyes darkening. "He's helping me get the Assembly Room ready," she said, referring to the room on the second floor of the building that was used for meetings, banquets, and parties. "The mayor has called an emergency town meeting for eleven this morning, right before the lunch rush."

Maya frowned, too. Ever since Mayor Wilson had been voted into office several months earlier, he had been making so many changes to how their quiet river community was usually run that it made her head spin. He was so different from their previous mayor, Mrs. Madison. Mrs. Madison was humble and honest. Mayor Wilson, on the other hand, was boastful and arrogant, and was happiest telling people what to do.

But perhaps Maya was being a bit biased. Mayor Wilson just happened to be the father of one of the most annoying and bossiest kids at school, Karla Wilson. She was always pushing herself into everyone's business and never gave a thought to the wishes of others. No doubt Karla would be right there next to her father at the meeting—a wannabe mayor, learning from the expert on how to be extra pushy.

"Who's that I hear trudging up those steps?" a deep voice called from the Assembly Room. "It's a good thing you're not robbers, otherwise you'd be caught red-handed with all that racket you're making!"

"Grandpa!" Maya and Nate called out as they dropped their bags on the landing and ran into his open arms.

"I missed you two," Grandpa John said as he gave each one a quick kiss on the head.

Maya admired her six-foot-tall grandfather. He was still strong and youthful even after working in his own freight company for many years. Buying the Library Café, named because of its historic connection to the tavern-turned-town-library next door, had been his retirement dream, and both Grandma and Grandpa were trying to make the quaint building into a thriving café and bookstore business.

"Your parents just called," Grandpa John said to the kids as he took their luggage from them and continued to the next floor. "They apologized for just dumping you on our doorstep, but they had to catch their flight to London." His green eyes twinkled in amusement. "Apparently *someone* wanted to take too many pictures of Independence Hall."

Nate, who was already down the hallway of the third floor called back. "I couldn't help myself, Grandpa. I needed to take photos of where our Declaration of Independence and our Constitution were debated and signed. I think I covered every square inch of the place that I was allowed to go to. I've got pictures of walls, halls, stairs, ceilings, and floorboards. We can have a slide show!"

"I was almost tempted to go along with Mom and Dad on their book-buying trip," Maya said, walking arm in arm with Grandma Georgia. "But I was so lonesome for this place, and our own home." She sighed, thinking about their two-story house a mile and a half away.

"Oh, we stop by the house every other day or so, to see that everything's alright," Grandma Georgia said. "But I'm glad you're back and staying with us for a week."

"Yes," Grandpa John said as he opened the door to the room Maya always stayed in. "You came back just in time to help us in the café. It may cost us a few more broken dishes as you serve and Nate busses tables, but we love having you."

"That was an accident!" Nate yelled from his room.

CHAPTER ONE

He scurried into Maya's room, his hazel eyes wide open. "I didn't mean to bump into Maya. You know that, Grandpa!"

Everyone but Nate laughed.

Maya tousled her brother's light brown hair. "He knows that, Nate. He just likes to tease you."

"Well, it's not *that* funny," he said with a hint of a smile on his face.

"We'll let you two get settled," Grandma Georgia said, linking arms with Grandpa John. "When you've freshened up, come on down to the Assembly Room. We still have a few things to set up before the town meeting."

"Who's running the café right now?" Maya asked.

"Mrs. Checagou," Grandma Georgia said. "And you'll be happy to know Maggie is here today to help with the lunch crowd while the meeting goes on."

Maya smiled broadly. Maggie, Mrs. Checagou's daughter, was one of her best friends. "It'll be so good to see Maggie again. I've only had a chance to talk to her a few times the whole month."

"Well, come down when you're ready," Grandpa John said.

THE SECRET UNDER THE STAIRCASE

As the two headed toward the stairway, Maya couldn't help but hear Grandma Georgia say, "Do you think we should tell them?"

"Hush, Georgia," Grandpa John said gently. "They'll know soon enough."

"What's with you?" Nate asked as he tried to skirt past Maya and go back to his room. "You've got a weird look on your face."

Maya yanked her brother back into the room and closed the door. Nate was about to protest when Maya whispered, "Something's up!"

"Yeah," Nate said, trying to push past his sister. "We have an emergency town meeting to get ready for."

Maya shook her head. "It's more than that. Don't you think it's strange? Grandpa and Grandma both knew exactly what time we were coming home, yet both of them weren't downstairs to meet us. And did you see Grandma's hair? When did you ever see her hair like that? Even when she's ready for bed it's *always* as neat as a pin. Also, I just overheard her ask Grandpa if they should tell us something."

Nate thought for a moment. "Hey! Grandpa never said, 'How's my boy!' like he always does when he first sees me... But what could be the matter?"

"I'm not sure," Maya said. "But I wouldn't be surprised if it has something to do with the town meeting."

"How do you figure that?"

"Because," Maya said seriously, "whenever the Wilsons are involved, there's bound to be trouble."

CHAPTER TWO

"Order! Let's call this meeting to order!" Mayor Wilson pounded the gavel rapidly on the portable podium that had been set up in the Assembly Room.

The crowd, however, was restless and wasn't paying much attention...until Grandpa John stood up.

"Folks," Grandpa John said calmly, "I know it's inconvenient to have this meeting in the middle of a busy week, but if we can settle down, perhaps we can get everything done by noon."

Maya observed the split-second, barely noticeable scowl on the mayor's face as the crowd complied with Grandpa John's request. She also noted the smug look on Karla's face when her father started to speak.

"Er...yes," Mayor Wilson said. "Thank you, Mr. Liber. First of all, I appreciate all of you coming on such short notice, but we have some important business to discuss that couldn't wait for our normal monthly town meeting. The issue concerns our wonderful school program."

A soft murmur rose from the crowd.

The mayor continued. "The council and I are enacting a new law. Starting this fall, your children will have to attend the school closest to your homes."

"What?" a few voices called out.

Maya was taken aback. This couldn't be.

"What does that mean, Maya?" Nate whispered to his sister.

"It means you can't go to your school and I can't go to my school either."

"But my best friends go to James Elementary!" Nate protested.

Maya nodded, trying to tune into the meeting, though she couldn't help but think this would mean she and Maggie, and their other best friend, Alex, would have to go to separate schools, too.

"My daughter and a friend will pass out the new boundary lines, showing the breakdown of the addresses and the school your child will go to," the mayor said as Karla and a stocky boy with spikey brown hair got up with a big stack of papers.

The boy was Otto Murdock, one of Karla's best friends, or, as Nate liked to call him, Karla's personal bodyguard.

"I see the mayor's got the goon squad out," Nate said softly.

"Shhhh," Maya hissed. "I want to listen."

Mayor Wilson pounded the podium two more times as more murmurs arose.

"This is for the benefit of our town…our children," the mayor declared impatiently. "We need funds to go to neighborhood schools. We have too many students going all over town instead of attending their local school."

"Here, doofus," Otto told Nate as he shoved a paper into his hands.

Nate scowled, but said nothing.

Maya grabbed the paper from Nate and looked over the map. Yep. Just as she thought. She would now have to attend Roosevelt Middle School and Nate would have to go to Hutchinson Elementary.

"But what about choice?" Grandma Georgia asked, surprising Maya who always considered her grandmother a bit more reserved than her grandfather. "We've always had school choice here in Kirkcaldy."

"Mrs. Liber," the mayor said in a slightly patronizing tone, "as a fine member of this community, I'm surprised you're being so…anti-teacher and anti-student. Obviously," he smirked, "this is for the benefit of everyone.

"But…" he said, looking sympathetically at the audience, "…because we know this might make a few uncomfortable—especially since some students are in their last year of school—we did make some provisions. A student can go to his or her school of choice *if* parents pay an extra 'fee' of sorts, an extra tax to cover expenses at both the closest school and the school of choice."

"That's extortion," Grandpa John called out, to the agreement of many in the crowd.

Mayor Wilson slammed the gavel down several times.

When he spoke, Maya thought the mayor was trying hard not to smile. "There, there, Mr. Liber," he said. "This really is not a matter for you. Your children are all grown up."

"But my grandchildren will suffer," Grandpa John said, trying to keep calm. "And since my son and his wife are out of town, I'm representing their best interests."

"Mr. Liber," the mayor continued, "you must know that as mayor *I* represent the best interests of the community. After all, I was elected. And we feel this is a matter that we need to implement. Think of the teachers. We need to keep them working. In fact, we had to shut down Whitefield Elementary."

"Why?" another voice called out. "Why was that school shut down?"

"There are some rules that weren't being complied with," the mayor said. "And we'll leave it at that."

CHAPTER TWO

The meeting went on for another twenty minutes with many parents trying to argue to continue the school choice program. But to Maya it seemed like they were wasting their breath. Mayor Wilson was not about to budge.

He finally said, "I think this is enough discussion for the moment. You must remember that it is out of courtesy to you all that we are even having this emergency meeting. We are trying to give you fair warning to make the process flow smoothly in the fall. And with that," he said as he slammed down the gavel, "this meeting is adjourned."

"Where are the teachers?" a woman called out. "Why aren't they here to tell us what they really think about this?"

The mayor ignored her comments as he put his papers into his briefcase. When the crowd realized they weren't getting anywhere with the mayor, many began to leave, but Maya could see that very few of them were happy about the meeting. The people who seemed the happiest were parents with children who had been assigned to the school which they already attended.

Maya noticed some townspeople talking to Grandpa John. But as the mayor headed toward the door, Grandpa John excused himself from the small crowd, and stepped in the mayor's way. Although Maya couldn't hear what was being said, she could tell that both Grandpa John and Mayor Wilson were getting into a heated debate. The mayor kept pushing his way out, but Grandpa stayed close behind, following him down the steps.

"So, what do you think, Maya?" Karla Wilson said as she came up behind her. "You can sleep in a few minutes later each school day since Roosevelt is just a block away from you."

Maya turned to face Karla. She was actually a pretty girl, with silky blonde hair and bright green eyes. But Maya felt Karla's stuck up attitude made her seem more on the unattractive side, especially when she had that silly smirk glued to her face.

"I always get up early, Karla," Maya said calmly, noticing Otto standing off to the side. "The day wastes away if I stay in bed too long. But I guess that means you'll get to rest, too, since your house is within Roosevelt's borders."

"Oh, no," Karla said, her smirk getting wider. "On the contrary, I'll still be going to Liberty Middle School. Being the mayor's daughter has its advantages." She smiled again, and headed out the door, with Otto at her heels.

"He looks like an overgrown puppy dog," Nate murmured.

"Arrrggghhh! She gets me so mad," Maya fumed. "And did you hear that? *She* gets to go to Liberty!"

"Well, look at the bright side, Maya," Nate said, always the optimist. "You won't have her to deal with either."

"It's still not right." Maya walked over to Grandma Georgia, who was starting to clean up the room.

"Oh, good," Grandma Georgia said. "Maya why don't you grab the broom and dustpan from the supply closet. Nate, you can help stack the chairs."

"Grandma," Maya began. "This can't be happening. I LOVE Liberty Middle School. It's the best school ever. I don't want to have to go to Roosevelt. They don't have half the academic programs Liberty has. And I love my teachers."

Grandma Georgia sighed, pinning back a strand of hair. "I know, honey. We heard rumors last week, and believe me, we aren't happy about this either. It had worked out nicely that after school you would come here since Liberty is just up the street. Your grandfather will do everything in his power to work things out. We could just pay the extra fee, but it's not right to do so."

"Why isn't it right, Grandma?" Nate asked. "Don't we have to pay for our schools anyway?"

"Well," Grandma Georgia said, "each town is different.

THE SECRET UNDER THE STAIRCASE

In our town, school taxes or tuition follows the student so that parents can choose the best education for their kids. But according to the mayor, if we want to send you to James and Maya to Liberty, then your parents would have to pay an extra tax, one for you and one for Maya, because you'd both be going to what he considers an 'out-of-area' school. Which pretty much means your parents will have to pay twice for the privilege of sending you to the schools they decide are best, not a school the mayor decides is best."

"Think of it this way," Maya told her brother. "Say you wanted to shop at O'Reilly's Hobbies."

"They have the coolest models and science projects in town!" Nate said excitedly.

"Exactly," Maya said. "You want to spend your money there. But suppose they made a new law and told you that you can shop at O'Reilly's, but first you have to give half of your money to Brewster's Toys and Tinkerings since their store is closer to our house, even if you don't ever go into their store."

"What? That's not right," Nate protested. "Shouldn't I be able to spend my money where I want?"

"Yes, you should," Grandpa John said as he came up to the group. "That's why this whole school choice—or should

I say 'no' choice—is so wrong. We've had school choice in
this community for years. One politician shouldn't be able to
change something so foundational to our community in just one
board meeting. Where were the public hearings?"

"Now, John," Grandma Georgia said gently as she
grabbed his hand, "don't get riled up. If only…"

"If only what, Grandma?" Maya asked.

Grandma shook her head, looked up at Grandpa John,
and shrugged.

Grandpa John smiled down at his wife. "I know, my

dear. Wishful thinking." He gave her a quick hug. "Kids, go on down and help with lunch. Your grandmother and I will finish up here."

"But…" Nate began.

"Do as I say," Grandpa John said quietly but firmly.

Without a word, Nate and Maya turned to go down the stairs.

But as Maya walked down the steps, she heard her grandmother say, "Oh, John. If only we could get the society's help right now."

"I know, Georgia," he said. "But you know as well as I *that* is just not possible. The society is over. That was then. This is now."

Maya walked slowly down the stairs. What was going on? What was the society that Grandma was talking about? Could it help them get their school choice program back? Maya smelled a mystery—one that she was determined to solve.

CHAPTER THREE

Maya sat on the east side of Memorial Mount, looking out over the town below. She loved Kirkcaldy Point. She loved how it was nestled between rolling hills with its quaint river town feel and its history as a small trading post in the days of early America. There were rumors that the town played a greater role in the fight for independence from Great Britain, especially since it was located along the Potomac River with the city of Alexandria to the north and George Washington's home, Mt. Vernon, further to the south. But so far no one had ever proved such a claim.

She saw the Library Café, attached to the Kirkcaldy Point Public Library, slightly to her left. Then she gazed over toward her own home across town, but her view was obscured by the many trees that covered the area. Looking out toward the point where the town got its name, she saw several sailboats gliding calmly along the river.

"I never get tired of this view," she said to her best friend, Maggie, who was seated next to her. The two had packed a lunch after helping out at the café, and had half-biked, half-trudged up the narrow trail to sit at the edge of the historical monument that had been dedicated to U.S. veterans.

"Mmmm hmmm," Maggie agreed, her mouth filled with chicken salad.

Maya crunched on a kosher dill pickle. "There's no better place I'd rather be right now than sitting here, chatting with my BFF, and enjoying pastrami on pumpernickel bread. What could be better than this?"

"Maybe you should go away on vacation more often," Maggie said with a smile, "so you can always appreciate what you have here at home."

"Maggie, I love our town. But something's wrong. I can see it in Grandma and Grandpa's eyes. What happened? We were only gone a month."

"It's Mayor Wilson." Maggie sighed. "I think he's power hungry."

"That's no surprise," Maya said. "What is a surprise is that he ever got voted into office."

"Well, he's getting worse. Do you know that I can't even take my dog Rexie to the dog park—the *dog* park—without having him leashed? That's what dog parks are for...so your dogs can run around freely! The mayor seems to come up with something new and ridiculous every week."

"Can't anyone stop him?"

Maggie shrugged. "You would think so, but since half the city council is out of town on vacation, Mayor Wilson and the remaining council members seem to be in a hurry to get a ton of things done."

Maya shook her head. She looked down on Liberty Middle School, which was two blocks north of the Library Café. She sighed.

"I don't want to go to Roosevelt," she said. "I want to stay at Liberty with you and Alex. Where is Alex anyway?"

"Mayuhnn," Maggie mumbled as she stuffed the last bit of sandwich into her mouth. She chewed quickly, then said. "He's in Maine. He won't be back until next week. And don't worry, Maya," Maggie said, giving her friend a hug, "we'll still be able to meet at the café after school."

"Right…after a sweaty thirty-minute bike ride to get there." Maya ate her last cookie and crumpled up her lunch bag. "Too bad there wasn't some way to get some help with this."

"Your grandfather doesn't have any ideas?"

"He's working on it. Grandma didn't seem so hopeful. In fact, she said something really weird to Grandpa as I was heading down the stairs to help with lunch."

"What did she say?"

Maya frowned. "She mentioned something about a society that wasn't around anymore to help. I think there's a mystery here."

"Oh, ho! Since when are you into mysteries?" Maggie said, laughing. "You're the one who's always mocking me about reading all those detective stories."

"See what a great influence you've been?" Maya teased.

"But seriously, I want to look into this society. Maybe they can help. But I don't know where to start."

"Well, in all the mysteries I've read, the characters have to keep their eyes open, considering anything and everything."

"Then that's what we'll have to do," Maya said. "Did you notice I said *we*?"

"Of course," Maggie said as she stood up and dusted off her pants. "I wouldn't let you go on an adventure without me anyways!" She walked over to her bike and removed her small backpack from the handle bars. "Oh! I completely forgot."

"What?" Maya asked, as she put her trash into her own backpack.

Unzipping her bag, Maggie pulled out a letter and handed it to Maya.

"This came for you in today's mail. Your grandfather told me to give it to you when I was packing our lunches. I stuck it in my bag, thinking I'd give it to you when we were riding up here, but I forgot. Sorry."

"That's okay," Maya said taking the letter. "I wonder who it's from." She glanced at the envelope. It was a typical letter size, white in color, with the security pattern inside so you couldn't read through it. But besides the stamp and

Maya's name and the café's address typed out, there were no indications as to who sent it.

"Now I'm really curious," Maya said as she tore the flap and removed a 3" x 5" card. "How did they know to send this to the café instead of my house? And what's this?" she continued, turning the card toward Maggie. "This isn't English."

The card read:

8-5-12-16 19-20-1-18-20-19 8-5-18-5:

5-24-16-5-18-9-5-14-3-5 19-8-15-21-12-4
20-5-1-3-8 21-19 20-15 2-5

13-15-19-20 15-14 15-21-18 7-21-1-18-4 20-15
16-18-15-20-5-3-20

12-9-2-5-18-20-25 23-8-5-14 20-8-5
7-15-22-5-18-14-13-5-14-20'19

16-21-18-16-15-19-5-19 1-18-5 ...

"It's a number cipher!" Maggie said.

"A what?"

"A number cipher," Maggie repeated. "I'm sure you've seen one of these before. Each number stands for a letter in the alphabet. We find the pattern and we can decipher it." Maggie took the card and turned it over. "Hey, this is one of those old library cards. You know, the ones they used before computers, where the librarian stamped in the due date on each line?"

"What book is it from?"

"*All You Wanted to Know about Secret Codes and Ciphers,*" Maggie read.

"Hey, maybe we're supposed to go to the library and find this book so we can solve the cipher."

"Well, unless this is a brand new book, our library doesn't have it," Maggie said as she handed the card back. "I know because I've read them all."

"I think we should go check it out anyway," Maya said, tucking the card back into the envelope and placing the envelope inside her backpack.

"You're the boss," Maggie said. "Lead the way."

They hopped on their bikes and headed down the hill, weaving past Liberty Middle School, Kirkcaldy Point Park, and several shops.

"We still need to find out about the society," Maya said as they pulled up behind the café and parked their bikes. "But I have no idea where to even begin."

"Maybe you can, you know, very *casually* ask your grandparents."

Maya shook her head. "And say what? 'Grandma? Grandpa? You know that society that you mentioned when you thought no one was listening? Well, is there any way you can tell me what the official name was so I can check into it?' I don't think so!"

"Okay, okay!" Maggie giggled. "I get the picture. We'll just have to give it some thought."

They made their way to the front of the building and entered the main library doors.

"Let me look at that card again," Maggie said softly.

Maya pulled out the card from her backpack and handed it to Maggie, who studied it again very carefully.

"If this is here," Maggie said, "and I highly doubt it, then we should find it in the children's section. The number is 652.8 GUA."

They headed up to the third floor, walked over to the nonfiction side, and began tracking down the numbers.

"652.8 FRA, 652.8 GAR... It's not here," Maya said.

"Told you."

"Well, hello, girls," Mrs. Shepherdson, the children's librarian, said as she pushed a cart down the aisle.

"Hi, Mrs. Shepherdson," Maya said. "Could you tell me if you have *All You Wanted to Know about Secret Codes and Ciphers*? I don't see it on the shelf."

"Oh, you won't find that here," Mrs. Shepherdson said.

Maggie gave Maya a smug look.

Mrs. Shepherdson continued. "It's over against the wall with all the other oversized books."

Maya returned Maggie's smug look.

"Thank you," Maya said cheerfully as she almost skipped to the shelves against the back wall.

In less than a minute she had pulled the book off the shelf and had it opened on a table.

"We're looking for the section on number ciphers," Maggie said as Maya began flipping pages. "Maybe we'll find a clue on which pattern they used for this cipher."

"Hey, Maggie. Someone left a sticky note. Do you think it's for us?"

The sticky note read: **ARE YOU READY?**

"Wow." Maggie scratched her head. "Well, I'm definitely ready to figure this out. So let's see." She quickly scanned the section. "Most of this I already know. Numbers are substituted for other letters, but we need to figure out what pattern to follow."

"How do we do that?"

"Do you have a sheet of paper?" Maggie asked.

Maya shook her head. "Only the envelope."

"That will have to do." Maggie took the envelope and one of the small library pencils, and began writing out the alphabet:

A B C D E F G H I J K L M
N O P Q R S T U V W X Y Z

"Now we just have to figure out which numbers belong to which letters. I think I'll start in the reverse. So A will be 26." She started writing numbers under each letter from 26 down to 1. Then she started to substitute numbers with their corresponding letters.

Maya in the meantime flipped through the book, reading a few paragraphs here and there. Cryptography was a very fascinating subject.

"Well, that didn't work," Maggie mumbled, still concentrating on the cipher.

"Why don't you try A as 1?" Maya suggested. "The book says that's a good one to start with."

"I'll try," Maggie said, "but that's way too easy. It must be harder than that."

But after just a minute she said, "Hey, you're right, Maya. That's the correct cipher."

"So what does it say?"

"Huh, that's interesting," Maggie said as she worked on the first line. "It says, '**Help starts here**' !"

CHAPTER FOUR

"You've got to be kidding!" Maya said as she turned the envelope so she could look at it better. "Did you decipher it correctly?"

"Yes, I did. And that's what those first three words say, "'**Help starts here**'."

Maya sat back in her chair. "Whoa. Who knows we need help?"

"Maybe it's someone from the meeting?" Maggie suggested.

"But this came in *today's* mail. Which means it had to have been mailed yesterday or before." She turned the envelope over. "The postmark is here in town. And it was stamped yesterday. But we weren't even in town yesterday, and we didn't know we needed help until today!"

"What do we do, Maya?" Maggie asked quietly. "This is too weird."

Maya sat looking at the envelope. Her mind was whirring with questions. Who could have sent this? Why was it sent to her at the café and not at her house? How well did this person know her and her family? Were they truly trying to help, or was this some type of trick? Maya wished she knew.

"Maybe we should just stop here," Maya said as she stood up, accidentally bumping the book and knocking it to the floor. "Oops!"

Maya bent down to retrieve it, but as she did, a card fluttered to the floor.

"Is that another card?" Maggie asked.

Maya nodded as she scooped up the card. It was the same type as the other one, but this time the handwritten words were in English and they said, "**Maya, keep searching**."

Maggie looked around. "Okay, are we part of some crazy TV show where the cameras come out and the host tells us, 'Smile, you're on Candid Camera!' or something? My dad found videos of that old show on YouTube."

"Obviously this is someone's joke," Maya said. "A person who knows me would understand that I would be skeptical. Let's just solve this, Maggie. Aren't you the least bit curious?"

"Yeah, but…"

"Look, we're safe here in the library. Let's just solve it and see what it says. Then we can go from there."

Maggie nodded and started working on the rest of the cipher. After about five minutes, she had the whole message deciphered. It read:

Experience should teach us to be most on our guard to protect liberty when...

"Does that sound familiar to you?" Maya asked. "Is it a quote?"

Maggie shrugged. "Never heard it before. And what's with the dots at the end? It must mean there's more to this message."

"Let's ask Mrs. Shepherdson about this. She might know."

The girls got up and tracked down the librarian, who was near the storytime area.

"Mrs. Shepherdson, can you tell us about this quote?" Maya asked. "Do you know who said it?"

The librarian smiled, put on her reading glasses that were attached to a silver necklace around her neck, and scanned the words. "It looks familiar," she said. "But I'm not sure where I've seen this before. Have you checked the internet?"

"Not yet," Maggie said.

"We wanted to see if you knew first," Maya added.

"Use the public computer by my desk," Mrs. Shepherdson told them. "Type in the first few words and see what pops up. I'm more than certain you will find it online. Just make sure you confirm the information with other sources. The internet is a great place for information, but it can also be a great place for false information."

"Thanks!" the girls both said and headed for the computer.

"You type in the quote, Maggie," Maya said.

Maggie sat down and clicked on the filtered internet connection. She typed in "**Experience should teach us**" and hit enter. A list of several sites popped up, each displaying the quote.

"Well, at least we know it's a famous quote," Maya said. "Who said it?"

Maggie clicked on one site, and then verified the information with several others. "The line was written by a Supreme Court Justice named Louis D. Brandeis who served from 1916 to 1939."

"What's the missing word?"

"The whole sentence reads, '**Experience should teach us to be most on our guard to protect liberty when the government's purposes are beneficent**,'" Maggie said. "But Maya, it's not a missing word. It's missing a couple of sentences. Maybe we're supposed to look at the entire quote, not just this little excerpt."

"Which is?"

"Experience should teach us to be most on our guard to protect liberty when the government's purposes are beneficent. Men born to freedom are naturally alert to repel invasion of their liberty by evil-minded rulers. The greatest dangers to liberty lurk in insidious encroachment by men of zeal, well-meaning but without understanding," Maggie read.

"So, what it's saying is that we need to be careful of those who think they can force you to do something because they have convinced themselves it's for your own good?" Maya asked.

Maggie nodded.

"That sounds just like what the mayor is doing with our school program," Maya said in a low whisper, looking around to make sure no one else was listening. "Do you remember he kept saying that this was for the benefit of everyone, or something like that?"

"The question is," Maggie said, "why did this person send this particular quote, even days before we knew we had an issue? And why to you?"

Maya shrugged, her cheeks flushing a bit. "Yeah, why me? What can I do about any of this? I'm just a kid. They must know I'd respond in a certain way, but what is that? What am I supposed to do with this information, now that I know?"

"Maybe it's a test," Maggie said, as she pulled out her library card so she could print out the page. "Maybe after you think about it, you'll know how to respond."

Maggie printed a copy of the quote and handed it to Maya. "But at least you have to consider one thing that's a blessing."

"And what is that?"

Maggie shrugged. "This may not be the society you were looking for, but it might be the help you need."

CHAPTER FIVE

"No way!" Nate said as he finished hearing Maya's story about the deciphered note. "This is so cool!"

Maya nodded as she sipped a glass of juice. She and Nate were sitting in the bookstore side of the café, Nate on a comfy couch and Maya in a leather armchair. Maggie had already left for her house some time before.

Maya placed her cup on a coaster on the table in front of her. "But," she confided, "we don't know what to do next. I don't think this was all this person wants to tell me."

"Why do you think that?"

Maya shrugged. "Call it a hunch, but if this person went through all the trouble of sending me a clue, then I think there's more. There's a purpose here, and I'm going to find out what it is."

"Well, I just hope it will help us with the school

problem," Nate said. "I really don't want to go to Hutchinson."

"And why is that?" Karla Wilson said as she plopped herself down on the couch next to him.

Maya almost laughed as Nate slowly scooted away from Karla. Karla didn't seem to notice that or the fact that Nate didn't answer her.

"Going to Hutchinson is nothing compared to what I think we should do to improve the schools this year," Karla continued joyfully.

"Oh?" Maya asked as she carefully folded the message and stuck it into the book she had brought from upstairs. "What did you have in mind?"

Karla leaned forward. "I think we should share grades."

"We're already in the same grade, Karla," Maya said, "although you'll be going to Liberty."

"Oh, no, silly," Karla said with a giggle that made Maya cringe. "I mean if you get a grade that's higher than someone else, then you need to share that grade."

"That's crazy," Nate told her. "What kind of idea is that?"

"A brilliant one," Otto said as he came up and stood in front of the table. He folded his arms, almost as if he was daring Nate to say something different.

Of course, Maya noted, that didn't stop Nate.

"So what you're saying," Nate addressed Karla, although he was looking up at Otto, "is if I had an 'A' and say, if Otto here was in my class—which I'm kind of surprised he's not—then I'd have to give him some of my grade to even things out?"

"Exactly!" Karla said excitedly.

"Well, for one thing," Nate went on, "I don't see why I would even want to share my grade to begin with, and for another thing, it wouldn't do anything to improve Otto's grades 'cause he'd still have a 'D.'"

Maya didn't like the changing shade of red on Otto's face as he unfolded his arms and tightened his fists. But when Karla shook her head, he slowly unclenched them, although Maya could tell he didn't want to.

"It's all very simple," Karla said. "Your 'A' is a product of everyone else's cooperation. Each class is taught by the same teacher, the students all interact within the same classroom asking questions and getting answers, and they all go over the same homework. So it only makes sense, and it's only fair, if we share the grade as well."

"I can see a million reasons why it won't and shouldn't work," Maya stated. "But I'll only share two. First, I'm the one putting in all the hard work and sweat to do my reading, research my projects, write up my papers, and take my tests. I *earned* that grade. No one took the test for me or did my work for me. It's my grade, not yours to play around with."

Maya leaned forward, placing her book on the table. "Second," she continued, "what if I study extra hard, but my neighbor doesn't study at all? You don't raise someone's grade by bringing someone else's grade down. Why would you punish someone for their own efforts, for their success? *That* would not be fair."

She stood up. "And another thing—and consider this a bonus—if I didn't do well on a test, most likely it's my own fault because either I didn't study or I failed to make sure I understood the material. I wouldn't even consider taking even a smidgeon of someone else's grade or points or what have you. I am responsible for me, and I wouldn't want it any other way."

Maya began to walk away, with Nate getting up and following behind.

"Nevertheless," Karla said in a rather cold tone, "I *am* presenting this to the school board when they meet on Friday, and I already have a few supporters."

"Good luck with that," Maya said as she continued on.

If Karla said anything in reply, Maya was too far away and too angry to hear.

"I think you got her mad, Maya," Nate said quietly as they headed up the stairs to their rooms.

"I don't care," Maya said. "She thinks she can push everyone around with her *brilliant* ideas. The only thing brilliant about her is the glare from the crown she thinks she's wearing."

CHAPTER FIVE

"Hey, Maya," Nate said as they reached the third floor. "Where's the message?"

Maya froze in her tracks as a wave of panic washed over her. "I didn't give it to you?" she asked, wishing it were so.

Nate shook his head. The two looked at each other, and then almost as one, they fled downstairs.

"I must have left it on the table," Maya said as they passed the second floor landing.

"Do you think Karla picked it up?"

"Oh, I hope not."

"But she wouldn't understand it, would she?" Nate asked as they reached the first floor and entered the café.

"With Karla, who knows?" Maya said tersely, moving around the café tables to get to the bookstore side.

Her heart, however, sank as she saw the area where she had been sitting not five minutes before. Her cup, which she had left partially filled with juice, was still there, but her book, with the message tucked inside, was gone.

CHAPTER SIX

Maya woke up the next morning with a headache. She hadn't slept well, partly because of the humid evening, and partly because she kept thinking of the previous day's events. She and Nate had spent over thirty minutes looking for her book the afternoon before with no luck. They had even asked Tom, the part-time bookstore clerk, if he had seen it or moved it.

Maya could only assume Karla had taken it, and with it, the message. Karla was observant enough to notice that Maya had placed something inside the book and then walked away. The book, which was a biography, wasn't important. But the missing message was. Karla couldn't do much with it, but the idea of losing something as mysterious as that clue, especially to Karla, made Maya feel as if she had betrayed the sender in a way. He or she had taken the trouble of creating and sending it and she'd lost it. How could she have been so dumb to leave it behind?

CHAPTER SIX

Maya sighed, rolled out of bed, and headed for the bathroom. She was already late helping with the breakfast crowd. She wondered why no one had woken her up. When she finally arrived downstairs, the café was bustling with activity.

The little café had had a thriving business ever since it opened several years before. Breakfast started at six in the morning, and lunch was served until two in the afternoon. Only beverages and desserts were available after that until closing, which, except for special occasions, was usually around nine or ten at night. Maya and Nate liked to help out whenever possible, which Grandma Georgia and Grandpa John always encouraged ever since they were little, even if it was only to set the table.

"You need to learn responsibility," Grandma Georgia would say.

"You need to learn about business and taking care of your customers," Grandpa John would say.

Maya just liked serving the people and making sure they got what they had ordered.

She was about ready to throw on an apron when Grandma Georgia saw her in the café kitchen.

"Oh, Maya, dear. I'm glad you're up. Are you feeling all

right? Nate says you were worn out yesterday, so we decided to let you rest."

"I'm fine, Grandma," Maya answered. "Thanks for letting me sleep. I do have a slight headache, though."

"You're probably hungry," Grandma Georgia said. "Go sit down at the front counter and I'll fix your favorite breakfast. In the meantime, pour yourself some juice and a glass of water, and take a few deep breaths. We need that circulation flowing to get rid of that headache."

"Thanks, Grandma," Maya said, giving her a big hug. She headed for the beverage counter, where she poured herself a glass of apple juice and a glass of water, and then sat at an open stool. Maya loved the sounds of the café: the clinking of utensils on plates, the hum of the hot chocolate machine, the gurgling of percolating coffee, the sizzle of bacon, and the chatter of the customers.

"About time you're up," Nate teased.

"Hey, thanks for telling Grandma I needed some rest," she told him.

Nate nodded as he placed a plate of whole-wheat toast in front of her. "Grandma said to start off with this."

"Thanks," she said, taking a bite of a buttery slice. "Mmmm."

"Hey, I've been thinking," Nate said.

"That's dangerous." Maya grinned.

"I'm ignoring that," Nate said as he leaned closer to his sister and lowered his voice. "What if Karla didn't take the message? What if Otto did?"

"Then Karla has it for sure now," Maya said as she sipped her apple juice.

Nate frowned. "I guess you're right. It's just that I thought he seemed interested in what you had to say about the grades."

Before Maya could say anything, Grandma Georgia came up with a platter of hotcakes and scrambled eggs. "Thanks, Grandma," Maya said as she reached for the syrup. "You're the best!"

"Oh, I almost forgot," Grandma Georgia said as she reached into her apron pocket and pulled out an envelope. "This came in the mail this morning."

She placed the envelope on the counter in front of Maya, and then headed back into the kitchen.

Both Nate and Maya stared at the letter sized white envelope in front of them with the name "Maya Liber" typed neatly across it.

"Do you think it's from our mysterious sender?" Maya asked.

"It sure looks like it," Nate answered. "Open it."

Maya picked it up and held it gently in her hands. "Too bad Maggie isn't here with her fingerprinting kit."

"Like you have access to a fingerprint database," Nate said sarcastically. "Just open it."

Taking a butter knife, Maya slit the back flap and pulled out a folded sheet of paper. She carefully unfolded it and realized...

"There's no message," Nate said. "It's just a bunch of square cut-outs at the top...or is that the bottom?"

"I saw something like this in the code book from yesterday," Maya said, ignoring his question. "It's a grille or grid or something like that. You place it over a certain page in a book and it reveals a message."

"Cool!"

"Wait a minute," Maya said as she squinted at the bottom left of the page. "This has a number on it: 37. We need to find the right book and put this over that page."

"Do you think it's from one of the books here in the store?"

"Who knows?" Maya glanced at the shelves that lined the right side of the room. "I wouldn't even know where to begin."

"There's my girl," Grandpa John said as he came up and sat on the stool next to Maya. "How are you feeling?"

"Much better, Grandpa. Thanks."

"There's a delivery I need done before lunchtime. Do you two think you'll be up for it after the breakfast rush?" he asked.

"Sure," Maya said. She and Nate were used to delivering books for the store.

"It's a devotional for Reverend Ferguson at the Old Kirk by the Scottish cemetery. He'll be in his office next to the old building."

"No problem, Grandpa," Nate said. "Where's the package?"

"It's by the bookstore register on the order shelf. You can't miss it. It has Reverend Ferguson's name on it."

"Okay, Grandpa," Maya said as she finished up the last of her food. "We'll take care of it for you."

"You're sure you're feeling all right? I can see if Maggie

will take a run with Nate if you think you'll get too tired."

"No," Maya said. "I'm up to it. I guess I was just hungry. My headache's gone now."

"Good," he said as he stood up. "I need to get back to work. I'll see you two later."

It was about an hour later before Nate and Maya could leave the café and head off on their bikes. From the alley behind the café they wound their way onto River Road, heading east. When they came to Crescent Drive, they turned left and followed the long curved road until they reached Old Kirk Road where they turned left again. The old Scottish kirk, or church, was to their right, with the old cemetery spread out behind.

"It's so quiet here today," Nate whispered as they headed down the gravel drive.

Maya nodded, and answered just as softly. "It's always quiet, probably because most of the people buried here don't have any more living relatives to come visit. This place has been around almost since Kirkcaldy Point was founded by Scottish immigrants."

They rode up to the office next to the old church, and leaned their bikes against an ancient looking tree. Maya opened her backpack and drew out the book, which had been wrapped in white paper.

Walking into the office, they were greeted by Mrs. Craig, the church secretary.

"Hello, kids," Mrs. Craig said. "Reverend Ferguson is expecting you. Go ahead and give his door a little knock and then enter."

"Good morning, Mrs. Craig. We aren't intruding on him are we?" Maya asked.

"He's doing some online research at the moment, but he told me to send you right in."

Nate led the way and knocked gently on the door. They entered when they heard a muffled, "Come in," from the other side.

"Welcome, children," the elderly pastor said as they entered the room. "Come on in."

The room, though small, looked comfortable and inviting. It had bookshelves along each wall, except for the big window behind the reverend's desk, which looked out onto a small patio with the old kirk in the background.

"Please have a seat," Reverend Ferguson said, indicating the chairs in front of his desk.

Maya and Nate both sat down. Maya held out the book she was carrying. "My grandfather asked us to bring this to you," she said.

Reverend Ferguson smiled. He took the package, thanked her, and then opened it up. "This is exactly what I wanted," he said as he examined the cover. "Thank you for bringing it."

He turned and reached behind him and removed a brown-papered bundle from a shelf. He extended it to Maya. "And this is for you."

Maya took the package, noticing a scraggly marking across it that reminded her of mountain symbols found on some maps. "Thank you, Reverend Ferguson. I'll make sure my grandfather gets this."

THE SECRET UNDER THE STAIRCASE

The kindly gentleman looked at Maya intently, his blue eyes twinkling with a mixture of amusement and seriousness. "Oh, it's not for your grandfather, my dear. My express orders were to hand-deliver it to you."

CHAPTER SEVEN

"Aren't you going to open the package?" Nate asked as they emerged twenty minutes later from the church office.

Reverend Ferguson had insisted they stay and chat for a while, even asking Mrs. Craig to bring them some homemade coffee cake to munch on.

"Not yet," Maya said softly as she placed the mysterious brown-papered package inside her backpack. "But I am *dying* of curiosity. Let's go down the block a bit, and then we'll stop. I just don't want to open it here."

"Okay," Nate said.

He hopped on his bike and rode to the street, with Maya pedaling close behind. They turned left on Old Kirk Road toward Crescent Drive and stopped under the shade of a poplar tree.

"Do you think it's from your mysterious messenger?" Nate asked as they both sat down on the curb.

"Who else could it be from?" Maya pulled the parcel out of her bag and set it on her lap. "And, Reverend Ferguson must know something. Did you notice how he avoided any other questions about the package and who gave it to him?"

"He's a pastor," Nate said. "They're supposed to keep... hey, what would you call it? It's not attorney-client privilege. Would it be pastor-something privilege??"

"I don't know, but I do know this is a book," Maya said.

"So open it already," Nate said.

"I will in a minute," Maya said, placing her finger on the front of the package. "I'm really curious about this design. What does it look like to you?"

"A doodle. It probably doesn't mean anything."

Maya shook her head. "No, everything about all this has been planned and carefully calculated. This symbol," she said, tapping the paper, "stands for something. I think it looks like mountains, but it could be anything."

"Maybe water?" Nate suggested. "Like a wave or something."

"Could be." She turned the package over and carefully pulled the taped seams apart. A one-inch thick book stared up at her. " '*Free to Choose*' " she read, " 'by Milton and Rose Freidman.' Never heard of them. Have you?"

Nate shook his head. "Is there anything inside?"

Maya flipped through the pages. "Nope. But here's something interesting that confirms this *is* from our mysterious messenger."

"What?" Nate asked.

She pointed to one of the pages in the front. "This is the exact quote we were sent in the first message, the quote from Justice Brandeis."

"Cool! We're on the right track. So what's the message say in this one?"

"I don't know," Maya said, carefully rewrapping the book and putting it back into her bag. "I left the grille upstairs in my room. I didn't think I'd need it for a delivery."

"Let's go then," Nate said, getting back on his bike.

The two made their way back into town. As they parked their bikes behind the café, Maya was a bit reflective.

"I still don't see how any of this will help us with our school problem," Maya said.

"Well, maybe we'll find out if we can solve this puzzle," Nate responded impatiently.

They walked in through the back door, entering the small hallway that separated the offices from the café and bookstore. A man of about sixty years or so, with a neatly trimmed mustache and beard, was exiting Grandpa John's office.

"It was wonderful to see you again, John," he was saying to Grandpa John. "Please send my very best to Georgia and the kids. Reverend Ferguson and I were just saying how long it has been since we've gotten together. Hope to see you soon." The man softly closed the door and turned into the hallway, noticing Maya and Nate right away.

"Well, hello," he said, clasping his hands together as they walked closer. "Are you enjoying this beautiful day?"

"Hi, Rabbi Mosheh," Nate said. "We must have just missed you before. Reverend Ferguson mentioned that he saw you earlier today. "

"He did indeed," Rabbi Mosheh replied, his eyes resting on Maya's bag before looking up with a grin. "We went for our weekly ramble. It's great to get out and about. This town has so many beautiful spots to see. In fact, perhaps you'll want to visit this one." He reached into his pocket and pulled out a photo of a large, rugged mountain-style home with lots of windows, overlooking a forest. "It's quite charming."

"Where is it?" Maya asked. "I don't think I've ever seen it before."

"You were almost there this morning when you were on Old Kirk Road," Rabbi Mosheh said. "If you had gone further down that road to the end, turned right on Mercer Place, and followed it about half a mile, you would have run into it. It's the only place out there. And it still has the most beautiful view of the Potomac. Here," he said, extending the picture to Maya. "This is for you."

"Thank you," Maya said as she took the picture and put it into a pocket in her backpack.

Rabbi Mosheh smiled again, his eyes twinkling. "Well, I'd best be getting back to my studies. See you soon, kids." He paused and turned to look intently at Grandpa John, who had just come to the door of his office. "Fare thee well, John," Rabbi Mosheh said quietly as they shook hands. "We're here if you need us." He walked quickly down the hallway and out the front door.

"Good, you're back," Grandpa John said with a smile, turning towards Maya and Nate. "Did everything go all right with the delivery? Did Reverend Ferguson treat you well? He didn't try to give you coffee cake, did he?"

"How did you know?" Nate asked.

Grandpa John chuckled. "Mrs. Craig is famous for her coffeecakes for church and town meetings. It goes without saying that he would offer you some. Are you ready to help with the lunch crowd? We'll just need you for an hour or so, and then you can go have some fun."

"All right, Grandpa," the two chorused.

"Great," Grandpa John said. "Maya, go put your backpack away. Nate, you go wash up so you can help set tables."

As Maya started up the stairs, she noticed Nate's look.

He was obviously anxious about what the grille would say. "I'll take a quick look," she said softly, "then head back down."

He nodded and entered the café. Maya hurried up the stairs, two steps at a time.

When she reached her room, she opened her bag and set the book with its wrappings on her desk. Then pulling the envelope she had left in the top drawer, she removed the grille. She opened the book to page 37 and placed the grille carefully over the page. It covered one paragraph, with certain letters revealed in the cut out boxes.

Grabbing a sheet of paper and a pencil, she quickly jotted down the letters that the open spaces revealed. She was a bit surprised by the message:

Visit Mercer Place.

Mercer Place? Maya pulled out the picture that Rabbi Mosheh had given her and stared at the large, light-filled cabin. "Whatever answers you hold," Maya told the photo, "we're going to find out!"

CHAPTER EIGHT

"Oh, why do I have a dentist appointment this afternoon?" Maggie moaned as she brought in a tray of dishes she had cleared from a table.

In between their duties both Nate and Maya had been telling Maggie about the clues they had found.

"Maybe we could postpone our trip and go tomorrow," Maya suggested.

"No way!" Maggie said. "You were out earlier when Mayor Wilson came in. He made an 'announcement' telling everyone there would be another emergency meeting this Friday—as in *two* days from now—to finalize the new school program. If you want to keep attending Liberty, we have to get some help, fast. And with what you told me about Karla, we can't let her get to the school board with her 'share-the-grade' idea, either."

"I just hope we don't find any more secret messages," Maya told her. "Solving them is your department."

"Well, you did a good job without me when you figured out that grille."

"That was only because I had read it in that secret code book the other day, otherwise I would have been clueless," Maya admitted.

"Ha ha," Nate quipped. "Clue-less. Get it?"

"Yeah, yeah," Maya said.

"Hey, are you sure that this house on Mercer Place is where we have to go?" Nate asked. "The clue said to visit Mercer Place. It didn't say anything about the house. Maybe it was just a coincidence that Rabbi Mosheh gave you a picture of a house there."

"You mean the *only* house there," Maya reminded him. "I don't believe any of this is coincidental. Now, granted, if we had been a few minutes later, Rabbi Mosheh would have already been gone, but, if he is in on this as I think he is, then he would have made an effort to find us."

Nate nodded. "Let me see that picture again."

Maya pulled it out of her pocket and handed it to him.

Nate stared at it intently, but couldn't find anything that stood out.

"Wait," Maggie said as she took the photo. "We always forget to check the back." She turned the picture over. The words "*Free to Choose*" were written lightly in pencil.

"Is that proof enough for you?" Maya asked Nate with a wry smile.

"Then let's hurry up here, so we can get going," Nate said as he started to wipe down the counter. "We have mysteries to solve!"

It was two o'clock by the time Maya and Nate reached Mercer Place, which looked as if it hadn't been used in years.

"I think we need mountain bikes to get through this crazy path," Nate said, swerving around roots and branches.

"Can you imagine driving a car down this road?" Maya replied, trying to peek past a bend in the road.

Nate shook his head. "No, and we don't even know if anyone lives here anyway. We were told to see a house, not a person. Hey, I think we're here."

Nate pointed to a massive rod iron gate supported by thick brick columns. A long narrow road, lined with beautifully maintained trees and shrubs, curved beyond.

Maya couldn't wait to explore. She opened the gate, expecting it to creak and squeak loudly in protest. But it opened in silence with surprising ease, almost as if someone had oiled it specifically for them. Maya paused to glance at Nate, who only shrugged.

"OK," she whispered, "what are we getting ourselves into?"

Nate just smiled and started to push his bike in. Maya reached behind her to put the gate back into place.

"Do you think we should leave our bikes here?" Nate whispered.

"We could," Maya answered.

"Let's hide them in case we need a quick getaway."

Maya laughed nervously. She could hear birds in the trees, and the gardens were absolutely lovely. But the silence made her uneasy. There was no one in sight. "Get away from what? We're here to see a house, remember? That's all," she said, trying to sound convincing.

Nate tucked his bike behind a large tree and some bushes. "This is as good a place as any," he said quietly.

Maya hid her bike, too, and grabbed her backpack. Then the two trudged up the driveway.

Maya stopped walking as she caught sight of the old three-story wood, stone, and glass mountain home, with its large decks and majestic angles. "Wow," she whispered. The place looked regal, even though she could tell the house had been built many, many years before.

They continued on and then climbed up the steps to the front door, gazing at the intricate woodwork.

"There's no doorbell," Nate said.

"This house is too old. You use that." Maya pointed to the brass door knocker in the middle of the door. The part that attached it to the door was shaped like an eagle, with a blank shield on its chest. The actual knocker, however, was a wreath of laurels attached to the wings.

"Pretty cool," Nate said as he lifted up the knocker and let it fall. He repeated this three times, the sound echoing throughout the house.

They both waited, listening for any footsteps. But none came.

"Try a little harder," Maya coaxed, not knowing if she really wanted to find out that anyone was home.

Nate rapped on the door again, but this time he held firmly to the knocker each time.

They waited. Still there was no sound.

"I guess no one is here after all." Nate moved over to the wall of windows near the front door and peered in. "What do we do now?"

"Let's look around," Maya said. "Keep your eyes open for a clue."

"It would be nice if I knew what I was looking for," Nate said with a frown.

They walked down the steps and headed around to the back. They found the garage, which was empty.

"I guess that confirms that no one lives here at the moment," Maya said softly. For some reason, she felt it best to whisper.

"Ooo Ooo Ooo. Ah Ah Ah."

The sudden eerie sounds made them jump.

"Wha...what was that?" Maya asked, searching for something, anything, that could have made that noise. "Was it even human?"

Nate shrugged. "Hello?" he called cautiously. "Is anyone there?"

"Ooo Ooo Ooo. Ah Ah Ah."

"Over this way, Nate." Maya headed behind the garage, trying to follow the sound. She stopped after a bit when the noise didn't continue.

"Where to now?" Nate asked.

Before Maya could answer, the sound repeated.

"Ooo Ooo Ooo. Ah Ah Ah."

Crash! Bang! Shatter!

"Eeeeyaaaah!" a voice called out.

"Come on, Nate. Someone needs help!" Maya cried as she ran through the trees.

CHAPTER NINE

"Eeeeyaaah eeee!"

Maya and Nate dashed toward an old shed tucked into the side of a hill. They burst through the door where a woman around sixty years old, wearing an old collared shirt and a pair of overalls, was sitting down on the floor surrounded by a pile of debris and broken glass.

"Are you alright, ma'am?" Maya asked, trying to catch her breath.

"Do you need an ambulance? The police?" Nate added as he bent to help her up.

The woman, who had looked up wide-eyed as the children rushed in, now looked puzzled as Nate brought her to her feet. Then she smiled, pulling out from her ears the earbuds belonging to her mini portable media player. "I'm sorry. I didn't realize I had company. Did you need something?"

Nate and Maya quickly looked at each other.

THE SECRET UNDER THE STAIRCASE

"We heard screaming," Nate told the woman.

"And then we heard a crash," Maya said, pointing to the shattered glass on the floor.

The woman looked down and frowned. "I've been doing a little cleaning up around here and I accidentally dropped a broken window pane." Then she looked up at the kids, her hazel eyes sparkling. "As far as the screaming..." she lifted up the portable media player where the sounds of a pop song could be heard from the ear buds. "I was getting into my song way too much. I'm afraid I'm a bit tone deaf, but I love music all the same. I always sing out loud when I think no one is listening. I must say I never expected anyone to be all the way out here today."

Maya, whose heart had been pounding from all the excitement, started to laugh. "I'm sorry," she said, trying to hold back the giggles. "I don't mean to be rude, but we thought…"

"You thought someone was trying to kill me?"

Both kids nodded.

The woman smiled. "I've heard it before from my late husband and my two sons. Don't worry, dear. I'm not offended at all. That's just the way God made me." She extended her hand. "I'm Eleanor. Eleanor Sloane."

Maya and Nate shook hands.

"I'm Maya and this is my brother, Nate. Can we help clean this up for you?"

"Oh, that would be very nice. Thank you."

She pointed out where the broom and dustpan were, and then showed Nate where the trash cans were stored. While the kids cleaned up, Mrs. Sloane chatted away. The kids learned that she was a retired teacher who had just returned from a trip to England, Scotland, and Ireland.

"You have a very nice place here," Maya said

"Even though this shed needs a *lot* of work," Nate said,

trying not to sneeze from all the dust.

"Oh, this isn't my home," Mrs. Sloane said. "This place belongs to a dear friend of mine. He's been away for a while and I'm trying to get him resettled."

"That's very thoughtful of you," Maya said. Maya really liked Mrs. Sloane. She was kind, funny, and didn't treat her and Nate like little children. She reminded Maya of her grandfather: wise, humorous, and respectful.

"It's the least I can do," Mrs. Sloane said. "Ben and I go back many years. In a way, I owe him my life." She was quiet after that, lost in thought.

"This is the last of it," Nate said, standing up from the ground and dumping the last bits in the trash bin.

Mrs. Sloane smiled. "Would the two of you care for some milk and cookies? I made a fresh batch of ginger snaps this morning and I'd love to share them with you."

"Yum!" Nate said. "That would be great. I'm hungry."

"We actually need to get back to town," Maya began. "We were sent to look at this house, but it doesn't look as if there's anything to see."

"You were sent here?" Mrs. Sloane asked.

CHAPTER NINE

Both Maya and Nate nodded.

"Is your grandfather John Liber?" Mrs. Sloane asked.

Maya nodded.

"So, you're the ones," she said softly.

"Pardon me?" Maya asked, not sure if she heard correctly.

Mrs. Sloane suddenly laughed, her face glowing with delight. "Please, you must come in. I insist." She headed out the door and onto the path that led to the house. Nate, with a huge grin, followed behind her and Maya followed behind him. Mrs. Sloane chatted once again, telling about all the old buildings and castles she saw on her trip. When they reached the house, she led the way across the large deck and through a small back door, entering a narrow hallway.

Despite the somewhat rugged appearance of the exterior, the interior was meticulously kept. Although there were moving boxes around, they were strategically placed, not strewn all over as one would expect. She brought the children into a room she called the parlor, sat them on a small couch, and excused herself while she went for the milk and cookies.

"She's quite a character," Maya said softly after Mrs. Sloane had left the room.

"I like her," Nate said. "And I like this house. I bet there are at least twenty rooms in here. And look at this crazy view. You can see the whole town from up here."

"But where is this mysterious Ben person? Why would he want to move out here so far from town with such a terrible access road? It's extremely isolated," Maya wondered.

"Maybe that's why he wants it."

"Maybe."

Mrs. Sloane came back into the room, loaded with a tray of cookies and glasses of milk. "Here you go. Dig in."

The kids ate ravenously. Maya didn't realize just how hungry she was, even though it was only 2:30 in the afternoon.

"These are great!" Nate said in between bites.

"I'm glad you like them," Mrs. Sloane said. "They were my boys' favorites. I can only make them in big batches, so it's a good thing you dropped by."

"Mrs. Sloane," Maya said, pulling out the photo Rabbi Mosheh had given her. "What does this house have to do with *Free to Choose*?"

Mrs. Sloane looked at the photo, turning it over to read the words written on the back. "*Free to Choose* was a book written many years ago by friends of mine, Milton and Rose

Friedman. Milton was an economist who taught about the relationship between freedom and economics, showing how individual freedom and economic freedom are tightly linked."

She smiled, gazed pensively out the large window, and looked at the town below in the distance. "Being free to choose what is best for you and your family is so simple, yet it's so important instead of having someone else decide things on your behalf. It may seem crazy, but there was a time when politicians and other officials were able to make random rules that forced you to buy or sell at prices they set. They prevented people from voluntarily participating and exchanging products and services with others who wished to freely participate and exchange with them."

Mrs. Sloane shook her head, then glanced wryly at Maya and Nate. "We seem to go through these topsy-turvy times every few years. People forget that economic freedom is the first freedom to go. They aren't prepared for the sneak attacks by others who wish to take over their lives. They're unaware that there are those around who are trying to deceive them by saying it's 'for your own good,' when it's actually not."

Maya and Nate were watching Mrs. Sloane with rapt attention. They glanced at each other in recognition as Maya said, "Well, this definitely sounds familiar." Maya then pulled the book from her backpack and turned to Mrs. Sloane.

"Through a series of clues, we were given this book and told to come here. Why?"

"May I see that?"

Maya handed her the copy.

Mrs. Sloane stood up, flipping through the pages. "This was one of Ben's favorite books. He had a whole library full of similar volumes. Come with me a moment."

With the book still in her hand, Mrs. Sloane led them to a room down a long hallway. She opened some double doors, and entered a big room that was lined with now empty bookshelves.

"Ben had such marvelous collections, even signed editions, including a few from Milton. Unfortunately, Ben experienced a setback many years ago, and he had to abandon most of his projects. But he's finally returning to town. And it's about time."

"I still would like to know why we had to come here," Maya said.

Mrs. Sloane sighed. "I can't answer that, Maya. Only you can." She handed the book back to her. "Dig a little deeper. Sometimes you hold the answers right in your hands."

"We better go then," Maya said a bit sadly. "Thank you for the cookies and milk."

"You're most welcome." She led them to the front door and walked them out onto the porch. "Maya," Mrs. Sloane said.

"Yes, ma'am?"

Mrs. Sloane looked at her intently. "Think of what you value most, and then think of what's beneath your feet. Don't give up. You are only steps away from finding the right answers."

CHAPTER TEN

"I don't get it," Maya told Maggie that night after dinner.

The girls, who had set up a last-minute sleepover, were sitting on the floor of Maya's room with all the clues spread out before them.

"Mrs. Sloane said that I had to dig deeper and that sometimes I hold the answers in my hands, which I'm thinking are all these clues. Then she said to think of what's valuable to me, to think of what's under my feet, and that I'm steps away from finding the answers, but I have no idea what she means by that."

Maggie frowned. "Of course she said that knowing already what you had to do. It's a little difficult on this end to decode her message."

"I know!" Maya agreed. "Nate and I have been racking our brains for the last several hours with no answers. We were hoping you could help."

"I don't know what more I can add to what you've done already," Maggie said, picking up the brown paper the book had come in. "Were you holding anything when she said that you sometimes hold the answers in your hands?"

"Sure. The *Free to Choose* book that she had handed to me. But so what? We had already checked it before."

"Wait, why did she have it to begin with?"

Maya shrugged. "I dunno. I guess she wanted to look at it. Then she got into a whole discussion of all the books that guy who owns the house used to have. She even showed me the room. It looks impressive even without any books."

"Would it have been possible for Mrs. Sloane to stick something in the book without your knowledge?" Maggie asked reaching for the book.

"Yes," Maya said excitedly. "She had her back to me as we walked to the book room. She could have easily slipped something inside."

Maggie was already flipping through the pages until she came to another 3" x 5" card.

"Well, I'll be…" Maya said, taking the card from the pages. "Hey! It's an old library circulation card for *Free to Choose*. But what does this have to do with anything?" She flipped it over. "There's no other writing. The only things on here are the book title, the authors' names, and the book's call numbers."

"It has to mean something, otherwise she wouldn't have hidden it for you to find later."

Maggie went back to looking over the brown paper. "What's with this scribble of stairs?"

"What? What stairs?" Maya asked.

"Here," Maggie said, pointing to the scribble.

"Oh, my gosh! That's it! Come on!" Maya scrambled to her feet and raced to Nate's room, opening the door without knocking.

"Hey!" Nate said angrily, but before he could say anything further, Maya blurted:

"It's the stairs, Nate! Mrs. Sloane meant the stairs."

"You mean the 'beneath your feet' and the 'steps away from finding the answers' meant the stairs?" Maggie said. "That would make sense."

"But stairs where?" Nate asked. "Here or at the house on Mercer Place?"

"It has to be *here*," Maya said. "Remember, Nate? Mrs.

Sloane said to think of what I value most. I value my family and this place. It has to be here."

"What are we waiting for then?" Nate asked.

The trio headed down the steps, looking for loose boards or for anything out of the ordinary. Finding nothing on the third, second, or first floors, they slowly descended into the cellar, which consisted of a series of storage areas below the building.

"Did you know, Maggie, that the tavern had its own ice well?" Nate asked as they carefully made their way down.

"Really? Is it accessible down here?"

Nate shook his head. "No. It's sealed off now. You used to be able to access it off the street. The ice was cut from the Potomac and stored in the well and used for drinks and such. Some was even sold to customers for their private use."

"I can't imagine not having ice cubes, especially in summer," Maggie said.

"Hey," Maya said as she pointed to part of the wall under the stairs. "I think I found something."

"What? What is it?" Nate asked as he and Maggie rushed to the area of the wall under the staircase that Maya was examining.

"Look here," she said. She pointed to something marked on the old brick wall. Scribed into the sides as if in outline were dark lines, climbing first vertically, then horizontally. Each line took up two bricks, making a rather large area that looked like…

"Steps!" Nate said. "Maybe it's a secret entrance."

"I bet that's what it is!" Maggie said excitedly. "Start pushing the bricks."

The kids began to push firmly on various parts of the dusty bricks under the indented lines, but nothing happened.

"This is frustrating," Maya said, pushing her hair out of her eyes.

"Hey, guys. Some of these bricks have numbers on them." Nate pointed to a few bricks with small numbers inscribed into the right corners.

"Here are a few more," Maggie exclaimed.

"What numbers do we have?" Maya asked, suddenly very excited.

"There's a 4, 7, 3, and 9," Nate called out.

"I have a 1, 2, 8, and 5," Maggie said as she wiped a few bricks with an old rag she found.

Maya grabbed another rag and wiped a few more bricks. "Here's a 6 and a 0."

"That's a standard set of numbers. So what?" Nate asked.

Maya's smiled. "I'll be right back!" She ran up the stairs, her steps echoing down to Maggie and Nate as she climbed up and up. A few minutes later, she was back downstairs, panting heavily, with two flashlights in one hand and the latest circulation card in the other.

"What numbers do you see on this card?" she gasped.

"The call numbers!" Maggie said, grinning in excitement.

"Nate," Maya ordered. "Push these numbers as I call them: 3, 3, 0, 1, 2, 2."

"Nothing," Nate called after pushing the numbers on the bricks.

"Bummer! I thought we had it for sure."

"Wait, Maya." Maggie pointed to the card. "We forgot the decimal point. The number is 330.122. We need to find a decimal point in the bricks!"

Nate and Maya looked around carefully at the other numberless bricks.

"Here it is!" Nate pointed to a brick to the left of most of the numbers. It had a dot in the middle of it. "This has to be it. Tell me those numbers again."

"Okay: 3, 3, 0, dot, 1, 2, 2."

As Nate pushed the last number, a small click was heard and the whole panel that looked like steps opened in, creating a door.

"We did it!" Maggie exclaimed.

"But what did we do?" asked Maya as she peered into a dark tunnel that disappeared somewhere beyond. Surprisingly, it didn't smell damp and moldy as she had expected. In fact, the walls of the tunnel looked smooth. "These walls are plastered," she said.

Maya flicked on one of the flashlights she had brought.

She handed the other one to Maggie. "Okay," Maya said as she saw the tunnel veer to the left. "Let's go."

Maggie turned on her light as well. She and Nate followed Maya under the staircase.

The air was cool, almost cold. Maya, who was wearing shorts and a T-shirt, wondered if they should go back and get sweaters as she shivered slightly. *No,* she thought. *We're already committed. We need to keep going.*

They turned left with the tunnel, and then right again.

"I think we're under the library now," Maya said.

The tunnel kept going, though now it turned left again.

"We must be beyond the property line," Nate suggested. "Do you think we're moving into the hills?"

Maya was about to say something when the tunnel turned right and they hit a dead end.

"It's another brick wall," Maggie observed. "Do you think this one has a code, too?"

They set about looking for numbers, but to no avail. They did, however, see letters.

"It's the alphabet," Maya said as they uncovered all the letters. "But what do we press? The name of the book? The authors' names?"

Maya, Maggie, and Nate took turns pushing in the various different combinations, but nothing happened.

Maya studied the card again. "Wait a minute. On the last doorway, we entered the call numbers, right?"

"Right," both Maggie and Nate agreed.

"But we didn't put in the call *letters*. The whole number with letters reads: 330.122 FRI. We need to put in…"

"F, R, I!" Nate said as he quickly pressed the letters.

A click was heard, and another doorway opened. This time, however, the tunnel opened up into a passageway made of rock.

"It's a cave tunnel!" Nate cried out, his voice echoing into the narrow chamber.

"Let's go!" Maya said, leading the way. The temperature dropped noticeably cooler, and she could hear drips and drops in the distance.

They had not gone too far before the tunnel opened up into a wide chamber about 150 feet high and 500 feet long.

"Wow!" Nate whispered, his voice bouncing every which way.

"Okay," Maggie said. "I think we need to head back.

I've heard too many stories about kids getting lost in caves. We didn't tell anyone where we were going."

"But Mrs. Sloane led us here for a reason," Maya argued. "She didn't seem like someone who would let us get trapped in a cave."

While the girls were discussing the matter, Nate had grabbed Maya's flashlight and followed what looked to be a worn pathway. "Over here!" he called, as the path turned a corner. "Follow the path."

The girls followed along, and the three soon found themselves standing before a door.

"A door? In the middle of a cave?" Nate said. "Now I've seen everything."

Surprisingly, the door opened at their touch, and they walked into a narrow, paneled hallway. Pictures lined the wall that led to another door, with a light shining beneath.

"Should we knock?" Maggie asked quietly.

"Might as well," Nate said. "It's too late to turn back now."

Tap. Tap. Tap. Maya knocked softly. Then loudly. No one responded.

THE SECRET UNDER THE STAIRCASE

Maya opened the door slowly, and they entered a round well-lit room. The walls were lined with beautiful bookshelves on all sides, except for one wall from which hung a huge display screen. Below the screen, standing about four feet tall, was a strange-looking old computer type machine. In the middle of the room were six comfortable-looking chairs.

"Now what?" Nate asked.

Before Maya could respond, the machine began to hum and blink, and then the display screen lit up, showing a young man of about twenty years old.

"Good evening, Maya, Nate, and Maggie. I am Milton. I've been expecting you."

CHAPTER ELEVEN

The kids stared at the screen.

"You couldn't be Milton Friedman," Maya said. "You're much too young to have written a book in 1980."

Milton smiled. "You are correct. I am actually a computer-generated three-dimensional image of Milton as a young man. And this," he said, indicating a young woman who had come up next to him, "is my wife and co-author, Rose. We have been programmed with all the writings, papers, books, and videos that Milton and Rose produced. Ask us any question. Our response will have a 98 percent chance of being similar to what the real Milton and Rose will likely have answered.

"We have also been programmed to maintain our humor," Milton said with a bigger smile. "It turns out I was a pretty funny guy."

Rose smiled and shook her head.

"Cool!" Nate said, getting up to take a closer look at the computer. "Who programmed you? What kind of software are you using? I bet you use up a ton of memory."

Milton and Rose laughed. Maya thought they both looked so real.

"We can save that for another time," Milton said. "Right now we have some very serious matters to discuss. You are not here by accident. You have been carefully chosen."

"Is that why we were sent all those codes?" Maya asked.

"Yes," Rose said. "We wanted to pique your curiosity. There were a few members who handled the actual delivery of those codes. But I don't want to get ahead of myself. Let me start at the beginning."

The screen changed and as Milton spoke, a series of pictures were shown. "We are part of a secret society that started before this country was founded. Our purpose: to preserve economic freedom throughout the world. Unless one is able to buy or sell things freely, or work for or even hire someone of his or her own choosing without the fear of force or retaliation, then people are not truly free."

The screen changed to pictures of people. Rose's voice continued. "Some of our members you may have heard of.

Others not so famous have been active members of our group throughout the years. They realized that America was a great proving ground for these economic principles, which have flourished here. But they are once again under attack."

Milton's image popped up again. "For hundreds of years, the society lived in the shadows. Forced into hiding, each member escaped in many cases with only a small traveling bag of priceless books and manuscripts. Now located all around the world, the members are hidden in plain sight—waiting. The Under the Staircase Society is starting up again, and it can only be led by young people, just like you three, who are committed to upholding economic freedom and, therefore, freedom for all."

THE SECRET UNDER THE STAIRCASE

"Is that what you call yourselves? Under the Staircase?" Maya asked.

Milton and Rose were both back on the screen. Milton nodded. "It all started when Adam Smith, a Scottish economist from the 18th century, delivered copies of his *An Inquiry into the Nature and Causes of the Wealth of Nations* to Benjamin Franklin in London in order to send those papers and others like them to America for reference and safekeeping. The secret passage that was used to move the manuscripts was under a staircase. Ever since then, that has been our symbol and our name. In many Under the Staircase locations, books have been preserved to make sure our ideals are saved for the future."

"I believe you visited Gunston Hall recently," Rose said as Maya and Nate looked at each other in amazement. "George Mason went to great lengths to hide the manuscripts from those who wished to discourage the principles of a free market society and economic freedoms. He built this secret area under the staircase as a replica of others found all over the world, and spent many, many years filling it with everything one would need to defend our cause. He even secretly received the valuable *Wealth of Nations* manuscript from Benjamin Franklin in Philadelphia, then quickly came back undercover by night here to Kirkcaldy Point, which was close to his beloved Gunston Hall."

CHAPTER ELEVEN

"You see," Milton said, "Many people don't realize that the *Declaration of Independence* and the *Wealth of Nations* were both published in 1776, the exact same year. Personal liberty, political freedom, and economic freedom—all available at the same time. It was truly an exciting period of history, and we owe those who chartered this secret society—and those who, at great personal risk, are willing to keep it alive—a great debt of gratitude."

"Kids instinctively recognize that economic freedoms and personal liberty are two sides of the same coin," Rose went on. "Your opposition to Karla Wilson's fair grades idea is a great example. Your grades—like wages and prices—are a measure of your time, labor, and expertise. You recognize that her idea is trampling your rights as individuals. And you recognize that she's trying to make you feel like you didn't earn your grades, that they're not actually yours. That way she can swoop in and 'redistribute' them to others. In the name of fairness and equality, her idea is actually very unfair."

Maya nodded in excitement.

"Exactly! Can you imagine if she took away some kid's bike? Or a pet? We would all be so angry. But if she takes away a kid's grade, even if it's just part of a kid's grade, for some reason it's harder for kids and their parents to stand up for themselves. To be proud of what they have earned. I mean, is it our property or does Karla think everything we own belongs to her?"

"That's a great question, Maya," Rose smiled.

"Mayor Wilson's school choice plan," Milton added, "attacks parental control and takes away competition that could help improve schools. With competition, good programs will survive and bad programs will fail. And by undermining parental control, Mayor Wilson is directly attacking personal responsibility, trying to convince parents that they do not have the ability and the responsibility to make the best decisions for their families. The irony is that his grand plan to improve education will ultimately hurt education. It will hurt the people he says he's trying to help."

"What could we do to help if we're part of the society?" Maggie asked.

"What you are doing now: standing up to ideas that squash our economic freedoms, which in turn squashes our personal freedoms," Milton said. "As my good friend Friedrich once said, 'To be controlled in our economic pursuits means to be...controlled in everything.'"

"Um, excuse me," Nate said haltingly, raising his hand. "Who is Friedrich?"

"Actually, Nate," Milton said, smiling, "You'll probably

meet my friend Friedrich—Friedrich Hayek—in the next few…"

"By the way," Rose interrupted, sending Milton a telling glance. He grinned sheepishly as he nodded his head in agreement. Rose smiled and continued, "You'll have lots of help in addressing these issues. You'll have a worldwide support system to back you up. The Under the Staircase Society will be there when you need it."

"We need to warn you, though," Milton said seriously, his smile fading away. "There are those out to destroy these ideals."

Rose nodded. "We call them the Distractors and you will see some of them encouraging all sorts of distractions that keep people so busy talking about the latest gossip and such that citizens fail to take the time to think and read up on things for themselves. The Distractors also try to prevent people from reading books about economic freedom. They don't want anyone to learn the truth of what is really at stake."

"So you see," Milton said, "there are some risks. You may face ridicule. You may be falsely accused of saying things you didn't say. Your opponents will always claim to have the best of intentions. And you may even be threatened. But remember, any freedom worth keeping is worth fighting for."

Maggie and Nate looked at Maya.

"What do you think, Nate?" Maya asked.

"We can't be afraid," Nate replied seriously. "We need to stand up for what is right. That's what our Founding Fathers and all the people who helped us win—and keep—our freedom would have done."

"Maggie?" Maya asked.

"I agree. We can't have people taking away the things that we value."

With a nod to her brother and friend, Maya turned to the screen. "Milton. Rose. We'd be honored to be members of the Under the Staircase Society."

Milton and Rose grinned. "Welcome," they both said together.

"You will not be alone," Milton continued. "You have already met a few members."

"You mean Rabbi Mosheh and Reverend Ferguson?" Maggie asked.

Milton nodded. "Yes, and Eleanor Sloane, too."

"Yay," Nate said. "We get her and her cookies!"

"And who is Ben?" Maya asked. "Is he someone important?"

"He is in charge of this area. He works undercover to protect his identity, just as you will. You will meet him, in time."

"You may be pleasantly surprised to meet some of our previous members, too," Rose added. "We know them as John and Georgia, but you know them as..."

"Grandma and Grandpa?" both Maya and Nate said together.

Milton chuckled. "Yes. You may inform them that the Under the Staircase Society is back in action. I'm sure they will be most pleased."

"That's really cool," Maya said, "knowing that they were involved in this group. But…what do we do about Mayor Wilson's program? How do we get out of Karla's fair grades scheme? They both have meetings this Friday."

Milton smiled. "Here is what we need to do…"

CHAPTER TWELVE

"Order! Let's have order!" Mayor Wilson pounded the gavel on the podium for the fifth time.

It was Friday morning, and Maya was pleased to see the Assembly Room packed to overflowing. She was nervous, though. Would Milton and Rose's ideas work to stop the mayor's school plan?

Milton had shared another quote from Justice Brandeis: "Publicity is justly commended as a remedy for social and industrial disease. Sunlight is said to be the best of disinfectants; electric light the most efficient policeman."

And that's what she, Nate, and Maggie had done the previous day. They made calls, gave interviews, and spoke to any and all who would listen. And from the size of the crowd, people did listen. There was even a camera crew from Alexandria set up in the back, ready to tape the meeting.

THE SECRET UNDER THE STAIRCASE

"Order!" Mayor Wilson called again.

The mayor, wearing what looked like a very expensive silk tie and a finely tailored suit, looked smug as he rapped the gavel again. Maya noticed that Karla was wearing a very pretty dress and matching low heels. She, too, looked smug with what looked like a brand new but fashionable briefcase.

When the crowd finally settled down, the mayor started the meeting. Maya couldn't help notice the little beads of sweat that were beginning to shimmer on his forehead. Hmmm. He wasn't as confident as he looked.

Glancing around, Maya recognized many of the people she had spoken to yesterday. A few of them gave her a thumbs-up. Then Maya noticed Otto. He was standing in the back of the room with his arms folded, staring straight ahead. Maya frowned, thinking of what Nate had suggested—that Otto may have taken her book and the message. It was at that exact moment that he turned to look at her. Maya expected to see his usual scowl. But to her surprise, he looked at her very seriously before giving her a small smile. Before she could react, he gave her a quick wink and immediately returned his gaze to the podium. Maya quickly faced the front.

"Do you see them yet?" Nate asked softly. He and Maggie were both sitting to Maya's right.

"No," Maya whispered back. "But Grandpa said he'd take care of it."

Nate nodded.

Maya smiled to herself as she remembered how excited her grandparents had been when they shared that the Under the Staircase Society was back in action, and that she and Nate were now members. Grandpa John and Grandma Georgia had even joined in making a few calls in order to get the word out.

After the Pledge of Allegiance was recited and the minutes of the previous meeting were read, the mayor opened up the floor for the townspeople to speak in either support of or opposition to the new school program. Many lined up to speak, including Maya. The butterflies that had been floating about in her stomach were now flapping their wings like mad.

A few residents were in support of the new program, but the majority was not. Mayor Wilson didn't seem to be bothered that his plan wasn't very popular, yet Maya caught him more than once wiping the sweat from his brow when he didn't think many were looking.

Maya looked toward the door. If only they would come, then she wouldn't have to speak. But as the minutes dragged, the line kept moving until she was next. Maya suddenly felt very tongue-tied.

Then she remembered why she was there: to speak out against a plan that would take away their right to chart their own path, to make their own decisions.

"Next, please," the clerk told her.

Maya cautiously approached the microphone. She looked down at Maggie and Nate who were smiling and nodding in encouragement. She glanced over at Grandma Georgia. Were those tears in her eyes? Then she looked out over the people.

"'We hold these truths to be self-evident, that all men are created equal, that they are endowed by their Creator with certain unalienable Rights, that among these are Life, Liberty and the pursuit of Happiness—That to secure these rights, Governments are instituted among Men, deriving their just powers from the consent of the governed.'"

The audience was silent as Maya paused. She continued, "These famous words are from our Declaration of Independence, and they remind us that our God-given rights are not established by government, but rather protected by government. That the power elected officials wield is the power we consent to give to them. That our elected officials must listen to us and not insult us by pretending they know what's best for us."

The audience cheered. Maya heard the normally reserved Mrs. Craig, sitting in the back, call out, "You tell 'em, honey!"

Maya smiled as she continued, "In the last thirty hours, my friends and I have made phone calls and visited many of our fellow townspeople. We have informed and educated them on this school program and how it will actually hurt us, not help us. Many were not happy that they were being *told* what to do with their children instead of being allowed to choose how their children should be educated."

Maya went on. "I know the mayor probably means well, but the decision of our education needs to be determined by our parents or our caregivers. It is not the government's job to force what is best for us."

Mayor Wilson began to protest, but many shut him down.

"Let her speak," one man called out, to the applause of several others.

Maya took a deep breath. "With a lot of hard work and with help from some friends, the citizens of Kirkcaldy Point have signed a petition that now has over four thousand signatures, encouraging the mayor and the town council to stop the mayor's proposal and to continue our education program as it has normally been, with choice."

The audience broke out in applause, with several whistles from Nate and a few others.

With a face red with embarrassment, Maya continued. "We are the governed. We are the people, as our Constitution declares, and we have a voice in what goes on in our community." She turned to look at the mayor. "With all due respect, Mr. Mayor, we want our schools back."

Mayor Wilson stood up. "And what if I refuse? I was elected by the people. I represent your votes," he said to the audience. "Are you going to let a child tell you what to do? I have your best interests in mind."

"Sit down, Frank," a voice called from the back. It was Grandpa John.

"We are in a meeting, John," the mayor said. "I will not sit down."

"Then I'm afraid you'll have a few people to answer to," Grandpa John said, stepping away from the doorway to allow the missing council members—Mr. Ross, Mrs. Elliot, Mr. Lee, and Mrs. Lane, the Mayor Pro Tem—to enter.

"Frank, you are so out of order," Mrs. Lane declared as she approached the podium. "According to Article II section 8 of the Kirkcaldy Point Code of Ordinances, you need two-thirds of the council members present before any vote, emergency or otherwise, can be cast and enacted. Your altering of the school program, then, is null and void."

"Yes!" Nate called out amidst the loud cheers and clapping.

"And furthermore," Mrs. Lane continued, "with the number of phone calls, emails, and texts the rest of the council members and I have received in regards to your behavior these last two weeks—not including calls from several state news agencies—you may be brought up for review, especially since a

few citizens are talking recall."

Mayor Wilson tried to speak, but thought better of it. His face was red with anger, but there was also an element of fear. He promptly sat down in his chair.

Mrs. Lane addressed the audience. "We know how important your children's education is. In fact, will the members of the school board please step forward?"

Several people stood up and moved to the front.

"I know this is a bit impromptu," Mrs. Lane said, "but the council members and I have been on the phone the last few hours, and we have agreed that it was a grave mistake to mess with your right to choose the best education for your kids. We will be back to school as usual come September, with the members of our community able to make their own choices as to where their children go to school."

The room filled with cheers. Maya was so happy that she gave both Maggie and Nate a hug at the same time, and this time Nate didn't protest.

"Mrs. Lane," one of the school board members called out. "We have been approached by a student—Karla Wilson, the Mayor's daughter—to usher a fair grades policy."

"Fair grades?" Mrs. Lane responded. "What's that?"

Karla Wilson stood up. "That's where students will share grades. It isn't fair if someone gets all A's and other students only get C's and D's. Since we are here as a community to learn, we should share our grades, too. This is for the common good of all."

"I see," Mrs. Lane said. "And what do you think of that, young lady?" she asked Maya.

"I think," Maya said, swallowing hard, "that each of us is in charge of him or herself. If I choose to study hard, then I deserve the good grades I receive. If I choose to slack off, then I am personally responsible for the lower grade I get. It is not fair for the one who worked harder to have to share with the one who didn't. We all have the same chance for a good grade. It is up to us as individuals to take advantage of the opportunities to be successful, in school or, really, anywhere."

"But what about the students who have a hard time learning?" Karla protested. "It's not fair to them."

"There is a lot of help out there, if we just seek it out," Maya said. "It's up to us to reach out and get the help we need. And you know what? We were all born with different talents and interests. Instead of being jealous of someone else's success, maybe you could cheer them on. Then you can get to work charting your own path. I know I will."

CHAPTER TWELVE

"Mr. Edwards," Mrs. Lane said to the school board chairman. "What do you say? Are you willing to take a vote right now on this so-called Fair Grades idea?"

"Madam Mayor Pro Tem," Mr. Edwards said, "the members and I have been discussing this issue at great length. We think students should be responsible for their own work and that the so-called Fair Grades idea undermines personal responsibility. We also feel strongly that students should not be at the mercy of the people who wish to have the power to decide what 'fair' means. Instead of begging Karla for their grades, we'll leave it up to the students themselves to make the most of their opportunities."

Karla sat down abruptly as another round of applause and cheers rose from the crowd.

"Then I think that settles the matter on today's agenda," Mrs. Lane announced. "We will hold our next meeting on our usual bimonthly date. This meeting is adjourned." She pounded the gavel down on the podium and the crowd slowly started to disperse.

Karla Wilson, however, was not so patient to get out of the room. She pushed her way through the lines and headed for the door.

"She's not too happy, is she?" Maggie said cheerfully.

THE SECRET UNDER THE STAIRCASE

"Hopefully we won't hear from her for a while," Nate said as he started to help clean up.

Maya frowned. "I don't think we've heard the last of her," she said. "Remember what Milton and Rose told us? We must remain vigilant because those who want to take away our freedoms never sleep."

Grandpa John and Grandma Georgia came up just then. Maya noticed Mayor Wilson talking urgently to someone she didn't recognize, before he, too, followed Karla out the door. The stranger turned to look at Maya. She shivered as his gaze swept the room, before he turned and quietly exited through a side door.

"Maya, you were wonderful," Grandma Georgia said. "John, you would have been proud of the speech she gave."

"I don't need to hear a speech to be proud of my granddaughter and grandson," he said as he scooped both in his arms, giving them a big hug.

"I didn't do anything," Nate told him as Grandpa John finally let go.

"Oh, no?" Grandma Georgia declared. "You were on that bike of yours yesterday so much, talking to friends and others in the town about what was going on. That *is* something!" She reached out and gave Maggie a big hug. "I'm proud of ALL of you."

"How did you find all the council members, Grandpa?" Maya asked, as she started folding up a few chairs.

"I had help," he said. "And here she is now."

"I'm so excited that everything worked out," Eleanor Sloane said as she came up to the little group. "And your speech, Maya. Very admirable."

Maya blushed.

"Oh, and Nate," Mrs. Sloane said, lifting up a white paper bag. "This is for you."

"Cookies! Thanks," he said happily.

"How about we treat you to lunch, Eleanor?" Grandma Georgia offered. "It's been a long time. I think we have some catching up to do."

"I would love that," Eleanor said. "Do you still have Scottish Lamb Stovies on your menu?"

"It's part of our Friday lunch special," Grandpa said proudly.

"Then let's go," Eleanor said as the trio headed toward the stairs. "What a way to celebrate a great day!"

"Hey, Maya. Isn't that the book you lost?" Nate said as he noticed a book that had been left on one of the seats in the back row.

Maya picked up the book and flipped through the pages. Inside, in the exact place where she had left it, was the message that had started their whole adventure. But who could have left it? She turned the paper over and noticed a little blue sticky note.

The sticky note read: **YOU WILL FIND HELP IN MANY UNLIKELY PLACES.**

"What do you think about that?" Maggie said as she and Nate looked on.

Maya shrugged. "At least I got it back." In her head she was thinking, *Thanks, Otto.*

The three slowly made their way down the stairs.

"I feel a little let down," Maggie said. "I mean, I'm excited things worked out the way they did. We'll all be going to our regular schools in the fall, and we can still work hard for our grades and keep them. But yet…"

"Yet you want something more?" Maya asked.

Maggie nodded.

"I feel the same way," Maya said. "But you know what? I bet now that we can meet under the staircase," she said softly, "our adventures are just beginning!"

EPILOGUE
LONDON – 1940

It's late at night, and a lone figure cautiously makes his way through the streets of the war-torn neighborhood. He finally reaches his destination and looks carefully around, hoping he hasn't been followed. Will the air raid sirens blare before his task is completed? He enters the two-story brick building that so far has escaped Hitler's attacks.

The house has been empty for some time, but the man knows he needs to remove a certain treasure that he's cached there and deliver it so that it will stay safe. The Distractors have been relentless during these war years, driven by the wave of evil that has swept Europe and threatens to go beyond the sea.

Downstairs, under the staircase, he faces a brick wall, and though he dares not strike a light because of the blackout, he knows which bricks to push, and he proceeds to enter the sequence.

EPILOGUE

CLICK. A brick panel swings silently away from him, opening up into a tunnel. Only after he has gone inside the exposed tunnel and closed the wall back up does he feel safe enough to turn on his pocket torch. He walks over to a wall, and removes a thick stack of papers. From his pocket he removes a folded piece of plain brown paper, wraps up the pages, and ties the package firmly with some twine. He pauses to reverently trace the symbol etched into the brown paper. He closes his eyes and takes a deep breath as if to prepare for the dangers ahead.

He heads down another tunnel, the light piercing the darkness. He hopes the route he needs has escaped the bombardments. After several twists and turns, he reaches another wall. He pushes a few more bricks, pausing momentarily to turn off his torch before he pushes the last one.

As he enters the chamber, he hears movement. Knowing that the room is rather small, he's on the alert, his neck tingling as the adrenalin flows through him.

" 'The curious task of economics...' " a familiar voice whispers.

The man sighs in relief. " '...Is to demonstrate to men how little they really know about what they imagine they can design.' "

The men clasp hands. "Hello, dear friend. It has been many years since we last spoke. Many thanks for your help."

"It is my pleasure, my friend. But we have little time. I'm late already."

"I apologize," the man says. "I was delayed. I have the package for you."

"Good."

He holds the package out, hears the rustle of clothing, and a pull as the package is removed from his hands.

EPILOGUE

"I will guard this with my life," the voice says.

"Thank you," the man says. "I hope it will survive."

"It must," the voice says.

The man hears movement, a click, and then silence. He in turn leaves the way he came, praying fervently that his package will get to its destination, to do whatever good it was meant to do.

ABOUT THE AUTHORS

I.M. Lerner

I.M. Lerner is a wife, mother, and small business owner with a background in marketing and IT. She loves to read econ books and articles for fun (yes, she is an econ geek), enjoys research, and is fascinated by what makes people tick. She is the granddaughter of Holocaust survivors and cherishes family above all else. She is a naturalized citizen who knows how absolutely exceptional this great nation really is. And she's writing these books so that our kids have a fighting chance. You can visit her at underthestaircase.com.

Catherine L. Osornio

Catherine L. Osornio has written fiction and nonfiction stories and articles for magazines, newsletters, and an early readers' program. Her first picture book, *The Declaration of Independence from A to Z*, was released in 2010. Catherine lives in Southern California with her husband and four children. You can visit her at www.catherineosornio.com.

Psst! Check out the Under the Staircase secret page at:

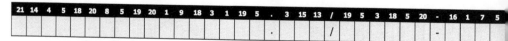

21	14	4	5	18	20	8	5	19	20	1	9	18	3	1	19	5	.	3	15	13	/	19	5	3	18	5	20	-	16	1	7	5
																	.				/							-				

Hint: Maya and Maggie decoded a similar message in Chapter Three.

Made in the USA
Lexington, KY
26 March 2014